Max and Molly's Guide To Trouble

Max and Molly's Guide To Trouble

How To Be A Genius

DOMINIC BARKER

ILLUSTRATED BY HANNAH SHAW

ORCHARD

To Carol
D.B.

To Holly
H.S.

ORCHARD BOOKS
338 Euston Road, London NW1 3BH
Orchard Books Australia
Hachette Children's Books
Level 17/207 Kent Street, Sydney, NSW 2000

First published in 2011 by Orchard Books

ISBN 978 1 40830 520 1

Text © Dominic Barker 2011
Illustrations © Hannah Shaw 2011

The rights of Dominic Barker to be identified as the author and Hannah Shaw to
be identified as the illustrator of this work have been asserted by them in
accordance with the Copyright, Designs and Patents Act, 1988.

3 5 7 9 10 8 6 4

Printed in the UK

Orchard Books is a division of Hachette Children's Books,
an Hachette UK company.

www.hachette.co.uk

Things That Go Bump In The Day

Max!

It was Sunday morning and Max Pesker
was jumping up and down on his bed
trying to bang his head on the ceiling.
He wanted to see if he could create
a **lump** out of nothing. It was an
IMPORTANT SCIENTIFIC EXPERIMENT.

Molly!

Molly was standing on a chair so she could see how close Max was to banging his head.

Come downstairs!

shouted their dad.

"Higher!" urged Molly.

"Higher!"

"Ow!"

Max succeeded in bashing his head on the ceiling.

Come downstairs, both of you!

repeated Dad.

"Do you have a **lump**?" asked Molly.

"Yes!" said Max, rubbing his head
and feeling a **lump** growing already.
"You *can* make a **lump** out of nothing."

I will NOT ask again!

warned Dad from the bottom of the stairs.

"I bet he does," said Max.

"Do you think I could hit the ceiling?"
asked Molly.

"No," said Max. "You're **too** little
and **too** young."

Molly looked sad. "That's not fair," she said. "I'm only twelve minutes younger than you."

Max and Molly were eight-year-old twins. But Max had been born just a little while before Molly. And according to Max, that little while made *all* the difference.

"I did a lot of growing in those twelve minutes," he assured his sister. "By the time you arrived I had almost **doubled in size.**"

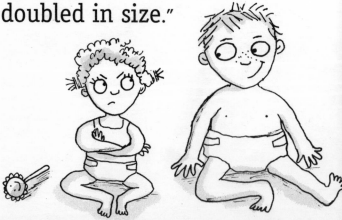

"Really?" said Molly doubtfully.

**Max and Molly!
I want you downstairs
THIS INSTANT!**

bellowed Dad.

"I told you he'd say it again,"
said Max.

"He is very predictable,"
agreed Molly.

THE DISCOVERY OF GRAVY

Max and Molly stood at the top of the stairs. Max had short straight red hair and freckles and was wearing a blue T-shirt. Molly had curly red hair and no freckles. She was wearing a yellow dress with stripes on. They slid down the

stairs side-by-side, face-forward, lying
on their tummies for extra speed.

"Don't do that!" said Dad,
jumping out of their way.

"Can't stop now!"
yelled Max as they
whooshed
down the stairs and knocked
over a plant that was
sitting at the bottom,
minding its own
business.

"Sorry, plant," said Molly. She picked it up and popped the leaves that had fallen off into the pocket of Mum's coat.

"Didn't you hear me calling?" demanded Dad.

"Yes," said Max. "You have a very loud voice."

"Then why didn't—" began Dad, but Molly cut him short.

"We were very busy," she explained, "doing an IMPORTANT SCIENTIFIC EXPERIMENT. We'll probably be **geniuses** when we grow up. You'll be very proud of us."

"Oh," said Dad. "Will I?"

"Already today we have discovered that if you bang Max's head hard enough on the bedroom ceiling you can make a **lump** out of nothing."

"Is that really SCIENCE?" asked Dad.

"Yes," said Max. "Isaac Newton was a **genius** because he made a **lump** out of nothing when an apple fell on his head. Straightaway he discovered **gravy**."

"**Gravy?**"

"It was an IMPORTANT SCIENTIFIC DISCOVERY," said Molly. "Before Isaac Newton, nobody had anything to put on their roast potatoes."

"I think you mean *gravity*," said Dad.

Max and Molly exchanged glances.

"Of course we don't," insisted Max. "First Isaac Newton discovered **gravy**. It was only when he was pouring it on his roast potatoes and he wondered why it poured $down$ instead of up that he discovered **gravity**."

"That's why he named **gravity** after **gravy**," said Molly supportively. "It's *obvious*."

But Dad still seemed unsure of the value of creating **lumps** out of nothing.

Max decided to reassure him. "Now I've got a **lump** on my head," he explained, "I'm bound to discover something very soon."

"Like what?" asked Dad.

"If he knew that already he wouldn't need to discover it, would he?" Molly pointed out.

With that, Max and Molly swept past their dad and into the living room.

QUALITY TIME

Dad followed Max and Molly into
the living room. Mum was sitting
on the sofa with a cup of tea and a
slice of chocolate cake, watching TV.
Dad picked up the remote control
and switched the TV off.

"I have been reading in a magazine about how we should all spend more QUALITY TIME together," Dad announced.

"I was enjoying spending QUALITY TIME with my cup of tea and piece of chocolate cake," protested Mum.

But Dad was not to be put off. He clapped his hands. "Let's all go on a

family bike ride!"

Instantly Max discovered a problem.
"Mum hasn't got a bike."

"And she hates exercise," added Molly.
"Yesterday we were in the car park
and she thought the pay and display
machine was too far away so she
drove to it."

Mum looked uncomfortable.

"Mum *has* got a bike," corrected Dad. "But it was right at the back of the garage under a broken lawnmower, because she hasn't used it since before you two were born."

"We're eight," said Molly. "That *is* a long time."

"Molly and I weren't born at the same time," Max reminded his dad. "I was born twelve minutes before Molly. Mum could have been on a bike ride while she was waiting."

"Trust me," said Mum, "the last thing I wanted to do in those twelve minutes was ride a bike."

"Anyway," continued Dad proudly, "I've rescued it, so now all our bikes are ready and we can be a proper family. Like the Goodleys."

The Goodleys lived opposite the Peskers. They were always doing family things. Sometimes they performed as a string quartet in their back garden.

"Let's go!" cried Dad enthusiastically.

Mum took one last longing look at her tea and cake, sighed deeply, and followed everyone out to the driveway where four bikes were waiting.

THE RIDE FALLS FLAT

The sun was shining in Trull, the small
town where the Peskers lived. Max
and Molly's neighbours were outside in
Laburnum Avenue doing the things they
always did on a Sunday – polishing their
sundials, talking to their radishes or

tuning their violas
(that was the
youngest Goodley).

Each of the neighbours looked a little
nervous when they saw Max and Molly
appear, but allowed themselves a sigh of
relief when they realised their parents
were with them.

"Are we ready?" said Dad, carefully
putting on his bicycle clips to ensure
minimal **trouser flappage**.

"Ready!" chorused Max and Molly.

"Then let's go!"

"Right. OK," said Mum, getting on her bike. Then she rode down the driveway and straight into a rosebush.

"Psssssssssssssssssssssssssssssssss!" hissed a tyre.

"Oh dear," said Mum, sounding not at all sorry and getting off her bike a lot faster than she'd got on it. "My bike has a **puncture**."

Dad arrived on the scene. "What's the matter?" he asked.

Max and Molly pointed at Mum's flat front tyre.

"Well, that's that. I can't go," said Mum, putting her hands in her pockets. "**What a shame.** You go on without me."

Dad looked disappointed. "But it won't be a **family bike ride** if you don't come," he said.

Mum didn't answer. She was looking in surprise at the leaves she'd just pulled out of her coat pocket.

"I know!" said Dad, perking up again.
"There's a **puncture repair kit** in the
house somewhere. I'm going to find it.
I've said the Peskers are going on a
family bike ride, and go on it we shall!"
He leant his bike against the hedge and
rushed inside.

"Well, I'm going back to my tea and
cake," announced Mum, and she skipped
into the house.

Molly looked at Max. "Shall we go and
see if I can bang my head on the ceiling?
I want to be a genius, too."

"No," said Max, looking serious.
"Do you remember what we used as
an ice-hockey puck last week?"

"Oh," said Molly.

"Exactly," said Max.

The **puncture repair kit**
had made an excellent
ice-hockey puck.

"And where is
it now?" said Molly.

"On top of next
door's shed,"
said Max.

"Should we tell Dad?" said Molly.

"No," said Max. "We don't want him talking to the people next door."

Molly nodded. There were a number of things which might come up in a conversation with the people next door. Max and Molly thought it would be better if Dad didn't know about any of them.

"So what should we do?" asked Molly.

"We'll have to mend Mum's bike ourselves. Now we're almost geniuses, it should be easy."

DEREK GOES SPARE

"Do we know how to mend a **puncture**?" asked Molly.

"No," said Max, picking up Mum's bike. "But I'm sure we can work it out. Remember, we are great scientists like Pythagoras and the one with the same name as me, Max Planck."

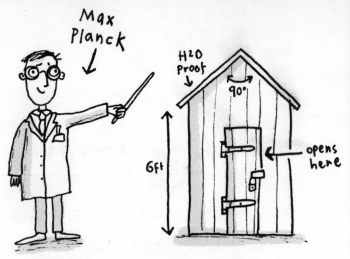

"Max Planck," repeated Molly.
"Who's he?"

"He invented the garden shed," said Max. "Before him there was nowhere to put the lawnmower."

Molly wasn't entirely sure that the garden shed counted as an IMPORTANT SCIENTIFIC DISCOVERY. Not like **gravity** or **jelly**.

"So how do we discover how to mend a **puncture**?" she asked.

"We do research," said Max confidently.

"What's research?" Molly wanted to know.

Max wasn't quite sure. "I think it means asking people," he said finally.

They set off down Laburnum Avenue looking for someone to tell them how to mend a **puncture**.

Almost immediately they spotted Derek. Derek was a short fat man with a moustache and a greasy T-shirt.

He was bending over the bonnet of his car, polishing it hard. Derek loved his car more than anything else. He spent every weekend polishing it until it was so bright and shiny it looked like it should be in an advert.

"Hello, Derek," said Max.

Derek didn't turn round because he'd spotted a tiny dirty mark and he needed to get rid of it.

"Why do you make your car look so clean when you always look so dirty?" asked Molly.

Derek turned round this time. Max groaned. Molly's habit of asking blunt questions was no way to get people to help you mend a **puncture**.

"What did you say?" demanded Derek.

Molly smiled sweetly. "I just wondered—" began Molly.

"How you mend a **puncture**?" interrupted Max.

Derek looked at them suspiciously.

"That didn't sound like what she said," he muttered.

"Didn't it?" said Max.

"No, it sounded like—"

"She was speaking a different language," interrupted Max again.

"What language?" Derek wanted to know.

"**Alien**," said Molly confidently.

"Alien?"

"Yes," nodded Molly. "They teach us **Alien** in school on Wednesday afternoons."

"In case we get kidnapped by a UFO and taken to a distant planet," added Max.

Derek was flabbergasted. "When I was a lad we only did French."

"So do you know how to mend a **puncture**?" asked Max, before Molly could say anything else to upset Derek.

"A **puncture**?" said Derek. "You don't mend a **puncture** yourself. You just get your spare tyre out of the boot and put that on instead. Then you take the punctured tyre to a garage to get it repaired."

"Thank you," said Max. "Did you know that the most poisonous creature in the world is a box jellyfish?"

Derek looked surprised. He didn't know that whenever Max wanted to thank someone or cheer them up he told them a gruesome fact from the natural world.

"One touch of its tentacles and you'd be in agony," added Max informatively.

Meanwhile, as Derek had been kind enough to help them, Molly decided she would help him in return. It was easy to see that the best way to help Derek was to do a bit of car polishing. She reached into her pocket, pulled out a tissue and began to rub it on the windscreen. Unfortunately, Molly's tissue wasn't very clean.

"Ugh!" cried Derek in horror. "What are you doing?"

"Helping," said Molly.

"Stop!" shouted Derek.

"I don't mind," insisted Molly.

"You horrible girl!" bellowed Derek. "You've put your nasty green snot on my windscreen!"

"It's not *my* snot," said Molly indignantly. "Our guinea pig has a cold. I can rub it off." She began to rub harder.

"No! You're making it worse!" yelled Derek. "You're smearing it everywhere! Stop, stop, STOP!"

Molly stopped. "I don't think you're

being very grateful," she said.

But Derek wasn't listening. He was staring in dismay at his smeary windscreen.

"This calls for **ultra-strong** cleaning fluid," he announced, and he ran up the drive and disappeared into his garage.

Max turned to Molly. "Derek said we need a spare tyre to mend a **puncture**. Have we got one?"

Molly shook her head sadly. Then suddenly her face brightened. "But

Derek has. He said so. In his boot."

"Do you think he'd lend it to us?" asked Max doubtfully.

"Oh yes," said Molly. "He's a very kind man."

"I know," said Max. "We'll find it, get it out, and when he comes back we'll ask him if we can borrow it."

"Good idea," agreed Molly.

The two children opened the boot and stuck their heads inside. They saw a spare tyre but it was obviously meant for a car.

"Maybe there's a spare bike tyre underneath," suggested Max.

It took all of Max and Molly's strength to get the heavy car tyre out of the boot. They put it next to the car.

"You hold on to it while I look," said Max. Molly put both hands on the tyre to stop it going anywhere.

Max stuck his head deep into the boot of Derek's car. He saw a bag of tools and a bottle of Emergency Car Wax, but he couldn't see a spare tyre for a bike.

"Have you found one?" asked Molly.

"No," said Max.

"Let me look," said Molly.

"All right," said Max, "but I bet you won't find it either."

"I bet I do," said Molly, appearing next to Max.

Suddenly Max jumped.

"What's the matter?" asked Molly.

"If you're here and I'm here," said Max, "who's holding the tyre?"

"Oh," said Molly.

The children pulled their heads out of the boot to see the tyre rolling steadily down Laburnum Avenue.

"What have you done with my tyre?" yelled Derek, emerging from his garage.

"It escaped when we weren't looking," explained Molly. "It's a very **naughty tyre**."

"Tyres can't be naughty," said Derek. "But children can." He strode towards them, looking very angry.

"Don't worry," said Max, grabbing Mum's bike. "We'll get it back for you."

Max and Molly charged off down Laburnum Avenue after the tyre.

Derek sprinted after them, shouting and waving his fist.

"You pesky…Peskers!"

CEDRIC GOES SWIMMING

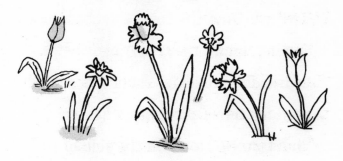

Mrs Meadows lived at the bottom of Laburnum Avenue. She was a smart and orderly lady. She liked to spend her Sunday mornings keeping her front garden smart and orderly, too.

"Aren't the daffodils looking cheerful,

Cedric?" Mrs Meadows remarked. She turned round to examine another flowerbed. "And the roses are positively blooming, aren't they, Cedric?"

Cedric did not reply. There was a good reason for this. Cedric was a garden gnome. He stood on the side of the small pond in the centre of the garden, holding a fishing line.

"And the dahlias have never been better, Cedric. Never."

Cedric continued to say nothing.

Aaaaaaahhhhh!"

There was a great shout.

"What can that be, Cedric?" said
Mrs Meadows, looking up in alarm.

Cedric continued to stare at his
fishing rod.

"Oh! Cedric!"

A car tyre was hurtling towards
Mrs Meadows. It was followed by two
children running at top speed, a bicycle
lurching between them and a red-faced
man with a moustache behind them.

This was not the sort of thing
Mrs Meadows had expected to see when
she moved into the desirable bungalow
at the bottom of Laburnum Avenue,
and she disapproved of it. Strongly.

Before she could so much as put
down her trowel, the tyre mounted
the pavement, bowled into her garden,
squashed her dahlias flat and knocked
the heads clean off her daffodils.

"Stop!" shouted Mrs Meadows.

But the tyre ignored her.

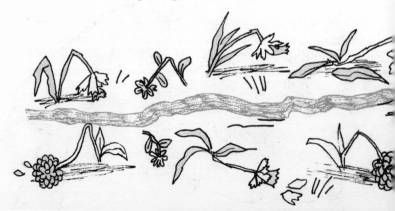

Instead, it careered across her
perfectly striped lawn towards the pond.

"No!" cried Mrs Meadows, shutting
her eyes.

There was a loud splash.

Mrs Meadows opened her eyes.
The large rubber tyre was lying in the
middle of her pond. Floating in the
water next to it was a gnome.

"Cedric!" sobbed
Mrs Meadows.

"Who?" said a voice beside her.

Mrs Meadows looked down to see two red-haired children looking up at her.

"I'm Max," said the boy.

"And I'm Molly," said the girl. "Who's Cedric?"

Mrs Meadows opened her mouth to speak and then closed it again. She was well aware that some people did not understand the deep bond that can form between a gardener and her gnome, and might laugh at it. So she said, "Never mind that. What I want to know is, who does that tyre belong to, and what is it doing in my pond?"

Max and Molly had always been taught to answer questions truthfully.

"The tyre belongs to Derek," said Max, pointing up the road. "He'll be here in a minute I expect. He's just stopped to take some deep breaths. I don't think he's used to running."

"And the tyre isn't doing much in your pond," said Molly, answering the second part of Mrs Meadows' question. "It's just lying there."

"Yes!" said Mrs Meadows in horror.
"Lying there with all of its oily ooze
seeping into my pond. Thank goodness I
don't have goldfish."

Max was a sensitive boy and he
could see that Mrs Meadows was upset.
"Did you know that a **black widow
spider** is the most poisonous spider on
earth?" he said. "Its venom will kill a
healthy adult in fifteen minutes. But for
children it would probably
be quicker."

To his surprise these comforting words only seemed to make Mrs Meadows angrier. "That sweaty man will be receiving a piece of my mind," she said, drawing herself up to her full height.

Max and Molly looked up the road to see that Derek had now taken enough deep breaths to continue chasing them. Even from a distance Max could tell that the break had not improved Derek's temper. He decided it was probably best to leave the adults to sort things out themselves.

"Goodbye," Max said to Mrs Meadows.

"But I still don't know who Cedric is," protested Molly.

Max tugged his sister's arm urgently and they ran out of Laburnum Avenue, pushing Mum's **punctured** bike in front of them.

"Stop those children!" yelled Derek.

But it was not Max and Molly who were stopped – it was Derek. Mrs Meadows stood in front of him, waving her trowel menacingly and demanding that he remove his tyre from her ornamental pond *immediately*.

There was something about
Mrs Meadows' grip on her trowel and
the steely look in her eye that made
Derek decide to do as he was told.

SNEEZY

Having run as fast as they could with a bicycle for five minutes, Max and Molly came to a stop and looked behind them. There was no sign of Derek.

"They've probably made friends by now," said Max, breathing hard.

"Yes, I bet they have," panted Molly. "And if it hadn't been for us they'd never even have met."

Max and Molly felt pleased. At school they were always being told to do at least one **good thing** a day, and introducing two neighbours so they could be friends was surely a **very good thing**. But they still had the problem of the **puncture**.

They took turns pushing the bike along Laburnum Avenue, debating the difficult question of how many handfuls of grass you could eat before you were sick.

Max thought about five would do it.
Molly said it was more like two. But both
agreed that if your handful contained a
worm you'd be sick more quickly.

Further along Laburnum Avenue, Max
and Molly saw their friend, Peter. The first
thing you noticed about Peter was that
his hair stuck up at the front.

"Hi, Peter," said Max.

"Achoo!" said Peter.

The second thing you noticed about
Peter was that he was always sneezing.

It was summertime, so he was sneezing because he had hay fever. If it was winter, he would have been sneezing because he had a cold.

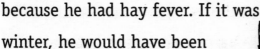

Peter was the unluckiest boy in the world when it came to colds. He was only seven and he had already had fifty-eight of them.

"Hi, Peter," said Molly.

"Achoo!" said Peter again.

"What are you doing?" asked Max.

"I was trying to hold my breath until I'd counted to a hundred," said Peter.

"Did you get to a hundred?" asked Molly.

Peter shook his head.

"You should count really fast," said Max, who'd spent years practising.

"That won't work," said Peter.

"Why not?"

"I can only count up to fifty."

Max and Molly saw that this could be a problem.

46, 47, 48, 49, 50 er...

"Then," continued Peter, "I try to remember what comes next and I forget to hold my breath and then I have to start all over again."

The three of them thought about Peter's difficulty for a while.

"Achoo!" said Peter.

"I know," said Molly.

"What?" asked Peter.

"Stop doing that because it's silly and help us instead."

"What are you..." began Peter eagerly, and then suddenly he stopped and looked around nervously.

"What's the matter?" asked Max.

"I'm still not supposed to play with you," explained Peter. "My mum said that you get me into trouble. She only got the last bit of my moustache off yesterday."

A few months before, Max and Molly had drawn a moustache on Peter with an **INDELIBLE** pen in order to catch a very serious **criminal**.

"We don't mean to get you into trouble," said Molly. "It just happens sometimes."

"Mum said that I'm **easily led** because I'm not very clever," Peter went on, "and that if you come round and ask me to play I should run into the house and shut the door behind me."

This seemed rather drastic to Max and Molly. But it did mean that Peter couldn't help them. Unless...

"We're not asking you to play with us," said Max.

"Aren't you?"

Max shook his head. "No. We're asking you to help us with an IMPORTANT SCIENTIFIC DISCOVERY. We won't be playing at all."

"No," agreed Molly. "We won't. And because the IMPORTANT SCIENTIFIC DISCOVERY will help our mum, I know your mum won't mind."

Peter still looked a little doubtful.

"*And* you'll be a genius," said Max. "Like us."

"Imagine how happy your mum will be when it says **genius** on your school report," said Molly.

"Is a **genius** better than a plodder?" asked Peter. "Because that's what it said on my report last time."

"Much better!" Max and Molly insisted.

Peter wasn't sure what to do. It seemed that whatever he did, he would get into trouble. "Achoo!" he said.

"He said yes, Max," said Molly.

"I just sneezed," protested Peter.

"Well it sounded like yes to me," said Molly, "so it counts."

"But…" protested Peter.

Max and Molly refused to discuss it further. Without knowing how, Peter had agreed to help them.

"Do you know how to mend a **puncture**?" asked Max quickly before Peter changed his mind.

"I think so," said Peter. "You have to get a pump and put air into the tyre. Then it stops being flat."

"Great," said Max. "Have you got
a pump?"

Peter nodded.

"Well, go and get it," said Molly.

Peter returned with a bicycle pump.
Max connected it to the valve on the
tyre and pumped. The tyre inflated.

"Wow!" said Molly. "You *are* a
genius."

Max tightened the cap on the valve,
then stood back proudly to admire the
mended tyre. There was a worrying
hissing sound.

"PSSSSSSSSssssss!"

Twenty seconds later the tyre was flat again.

"The air must have escaped through a **hole**," said Peter.

"I can't see a **hole**," said Max.

"Air can get out of a really tiny **hole**," said Peter.

"Air is stupid," said Molly. "It's too small and you don't know where it is. It would be much better to put something in the tyre that couldn't get out of a tiny **hole**."

"You're right," agreed Max.
"But what?"

"We had a **hole** in our garden once,"
said Peter.

"How did you get rid of it?" asked
Molly.

"We filled it up with soil."

"Maybe that's how we should mend
the tyre," suggested Max.

"I bet it is," said Molly. "And when
we've done it we'll be able to tell
everyone else and then everyone will

put mud in their tyres instead of
air and nobody will ever have any
punctures again."

"Wow!" said Peter.

"It will be our second IMPORTANT
SCIENTIFIC DISCOVERY as
geniuses," Molly added.

"Second?" asked Peter.

Proudly, Molly pointed to the **lump**
on top of Max's head.

THE HOLE STORY

Half an hour later Max and Molly had dug a large **hole** in a flowerbed in Peter's front garden. They put the soil in a bucket Peter had found in the garage.

But in the last few minutes Peter had begun to look anxious. "That is quite a big **hole**," he said.

Molly thought about Mrs Meadows'
garden. "It could be a pond," she
suggested.

"I'm not sure my mum wants a pond,"
said Peter doubtfully. "And she'll be
back from the hairdresser's soon."

Molly held up her hand. "Don't
worry," she said.

"It's all right for you," said Peter.
"You're not the one who's got to
explain a great big **hole** in your
mum's flowerbed."

"We could put a cover over it so she won't see it," suggested Max. "Then we'll fill it up again later."

"But she'll just look under the cover," said Peter.

"We could put some soil on the cover," said Molly. "Then it will be hidden."

Peter looked at the large **hole** in the middle of his mum's best flowerbed and decided it was worth a try. He found an old bit of tarpaulin in the garage which they spread over the **hole**. Then they sprinkled soil on top.

"There," said Molly, pleased. "Nobody would know."

"Not like standing on a stonefish," observed Max. "If you did that *everybody* would know."

THE WHEEL GOES UNROUND

Although they all agreed that Peter's mum would absolutely want Peter to help them, the children felt that it might be best if she didn't see them together. After all, she wouldn't know that they weren't playing, and she might leap to the wrong conclusion and tell them off. To save her the embarrassment of having to apologise when she discovered the truth, they decided to go and mend the **puncture** somewhere else.

Max led the way out of Laburnum Avenue, pushing the bike, followed by Peter carrying the bucket of soil. Molly skipped alongside to distract him from how heavy it was. She could have

helped him carry it, but that didn't
seem like the kind of creative solution
that a genius would come
up with.

They trudged along Park Road,
across Chestnut Terrace and right up
Hill Rise, which was the highest road
in Trull.

"We'll mend it here," announced Max,
dropping the bike.

"OK," agreed Peter, putting down
the bucket.

"What do we do?" asked Molly.

Max looked at the flat tyre. "We fill it up with soil," he said.

"We need a **hole** to push the soil into," said Peter.

"But there isn't a **hole**," observed Molly.

They studied the tyre closely. Molly was right. There still wasn't a **hole**.

"I know," said Max suddenly. "If we pull the tyre off the wheel a bit then there will be enough of a gap to push the soil in."

Using all the strength in his fingers, Max pulled the tyre

away from the rim of the wheel. Peter squashed as much soil as he could into the gap between the tyre and the rim. Molly made herself useful by supervising. She'd always been good at telling everybody else what to do.

"Pull it back more," she told Max. "Squidge more soil in," she told Peter.

It was hard work, but slowly the tyre began to fill up with mud until at last, with Molly's encouragement, it was completely full.

"I can't get any more in," said Peter, wiping his filthy fingers on his T-shirt.

The three children looked at the tyre. It certainly wasn't flat any more. But it wasn't perfectly round either – it was...

...lumpy.

"I'm not sure it looks right," said
Peter uncertainly.

"Not yet, it doesn't," said Molly
confidently. "It just needs a bit of riding
to smooth it out."

"Does it?" asked Peter.

"Yes," insisted Molly. "So get on it and
ride it."

"I'm too small," protested Peter.
"I won't be able to reach the pedals."

Peter had identified a problem. None
of them was big enough to ride the bike.

"It doesn't matter," Max assured him.

"You're only going downhill so you don't need to reach the pedals. You just need to sit on the seat and reach the handlebars and the brakes."

"But—" began Peter, who wasn't sure how he had ended up being chosen to do the first test ride.

"Peter," interrupted Molly sternly. "You do want to help SCIENCE and be a genius, don't you?"

"Achoo!" said Peter.

"I knew you did," beamed Molly.

And before Peter could object again,

Max and Molly were heaving him onto
the bike.

"Just freewheel down to the bottom of
the hill and stop," said Max. "It's easy."

"We'll run after you," said Molly.

They both gave the bike a push.

"Achoo, achoo, achoo!"
said Peter, who sneezed more when he
was nervous. Within seconds he had
disappeared over the brow of the hill.

HOOLIGAN LEGS

Old Mr Everett was walking his dog,
Snowy, up Hill Rise. It was part of the
same walk that was part of the same
routine that was part of the same
day that Old Mr Everett had enjoyed
ever since he'd retired as a postman.

And every morning before he set off, he would clean and brush Snowy thoroughly.

"Come on, lad," he said to Snowy. "Let's be getting up to the top of this hill. Then we head back home for a cup of tea for me and some dog biscuits for you."

"Achoo, achoo, achoo!"

Old Mr Everett looked up the road. Zigzagging crazily down it was a boy on a bicycle that was far too big for him, with mud shooting out of its front tyre in all directions. He was being chased by two other children running at top speed.

"What's this, Snowy?" said Old Mr Everett, peering through his glasses.

Whatever it was, it was getting more and more out of control.

"Achoo! *Achoo!*" The boy veered wildly and headed straight for Old Mr Everett and Snowy.

"Woah!" cried Old Mr Everett.

"Help!" shouted the boy.

But the boy was beyond help. Spewing out more and more soil, the bike sped past Old Mr Everett, missing him by millimetres, and crashed straight into

the hedge behind him. The rider
shot over the handlebars and landed
head-first in the hedge with his legs
sticking out.

Old Mr Everett looked down at Snowy.
The bike may have missed them but
the mud had not. Snowy was muddy.
Very muddy.

"Help!" said the legs, waving wildly.

"Look what you've done to my dog!" shouted Old Mr Everett.

"I can't!" said the legs.

The two children who had been chasing the bike arrived, panting.

"Hello," said the girl. "I'm Molly and this is Max. And those are Peter's legs."

"Look what he's done to my dog!" repeated Old Mr Everett.

Max could see that Old Mr Everett was not happy. "Did you know that the **golden poison dart frog** has

enough venom to kill twenty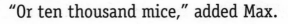
people?" he said politely.

Old Mr Everett looked
puzzled.

"Or ten thousand mice," added Max.

"Help!" shouted the legs again.
"Achoo!"

Max and Molly reached up, grabbed
one of Peter's legs each and pulled.
Peter emerged with a number of twigs
attached to his hair.

The sight of him brought Old Mr
Everett back to his senses. "You're a

hooligan!" he shouted, brandishing his shopping bag threateningly. "You're all hooligans!"

"Not all of us," corrected Molly quickly. "Only Peter is really a hooligan."

"Achoo!" sneezed Peter. "Am I?"

"Yes," said Molly. "You are a hooligan because you sprayed mud all over Old Mr Everett's dog. You should be ashamed of yourself."

"But..." Peter couldn't believe what he was hearing.

"He should have an **ASBO**," said Old Mr Everett, lowering his shopping bag. "Or an electronic tag."

"Or both," suggested Max.

Peter was speechless. But Molly wasn't.

"He should," she agreed. "But we're going to give him one last chance to mend his ways."

"Are we?" said Old Mr Everett dubiously.

"We are," said Molly. "He's going to wash your dog so that he's all white again. And we'll help him to make sure he does it properly."

"Maybe I should just call the police," suggested Old Mr Everett. "Or at least tell his parents."

"I wouldn't," said Molly hastily. "He's had a very hard life."

"Has he?" asked Old Mr Everett.

"Achoo!" said Peter.

"Lots of colds," explained Molly.

Old Mr Everett was a kind man who didn't really want to phone the police. Especially now he knew that somebody

was going to clean his dog. He gave
Peter a stern look.

"You're a very lucky young man to
have friends who stick up for you,"
said Old Mr Everett. "I'm going to give
you a chance to make amends for what
you've done."

Peter sneezed.

"Have you washed a dog before?"
Old Mr Everett asked him.

Peter hadn't. He didn't know what
to say.

Fortunately, Molly did.

"We've washed our dog Spotty lots
of times," she said.

Old Mr Everett looked relieved. Perhaps
he wouldn't have done if he'd noticed
the look of surprise on Max's face.

"Do you know how to mend a
puncture?" asked Molly.

"Forty years as a postman?
Course I know how to mend
a **puncture**."

BATH TIME!

Max, Molly and Peter were standing in
Old Mr Everett's back garden. Molly was
filling an old bath full of water with a
hosepipe. Max and Peter were holding
Snowy. Snowy watched the bath filling
up and had a good idea of what was

about to happen next. Unfortunately for Max and Molly, he didn't like baths.

"Good dog, Snowy," said Max.

But Snowy was not a dog to be won over by flattery. He struggled to escape from Max and Peter's grasp.

"Hurry up with the water, Molly," urged Max.

"I can't make it go any faster!"

Inside his garage Old Mr Everett was mending the **puncture** on Mum's bike.

"We have to get Snowy clean before Old Mr Everett's finished," said Max.

The bath was almost full.

"That's enough," said Max. "Get the brush and the soap."

Molly dropped the hose and went to get the brush and the soap that Old Mr Everett had left on the decking underneath his pergola.

"Come on, Snowy," said Peter soothingly. "Nice clean water."

Snowy growled at the water.

"We're going to have to lift him in," said Max. "Ready! Steady! Go!"

Max and Peter lifted Snowy up.

"Put him in the bath!" said Molly.

But Snowy was not going in the bath.
Just as Max and Peter were about to
lower him in, he squirmed free and leapt
over it. Peter wasn't so lucky. With a
yelp, he overbalanced and tumbled into
the bath with a **splash**.

When he reappeared his hair no longer
stuck up at the front. It was plastered
to the side of his head.

"Achoo!"

"What are you doing, Peter?" demanded Molly. "I'm not going to wash *you*."

"Get out of the bath and help us catch Snowy!" said Max.

The three children chased Snowy round the garden. Snowy thought this was great. Much more fun than having a bath. He raced across the lawn, through the flowerbeds, past the pots,

 back and forth across the decking and finally into the greenhouse where

Old Mr Everett grew his prize tomatoes.

"Quick!" said Max. "We've got him!"

Which showed how much Max knew. They could have chased Snowy for the whole day and never caught him. The only thing that was going to stop Snowy was the voice of Old Mr Everett. Which was exactly what he heard next.

"What's going on?" shouted Old Mr Everett, emerging from the garage with the newly repaired bike. He stopped in his tracks. "What have you done to my garden?"

Snowy stopped. So did Max, Molly and Peter. They saw the chaos their chase had caused in the garden. Flowers were trampled, pots were overturned and the decking was covered in muddy pawprints and squashed prize tomatoes.

"I thought you were going to wash my dog, not ruin my garden!" said

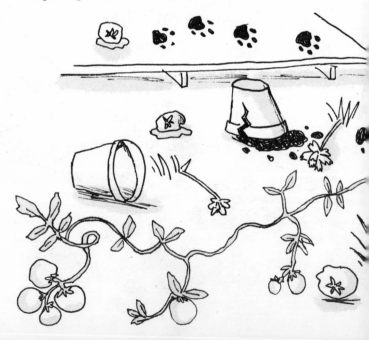

Old Mr Everett. "He's **dirtier** than he was before!"

Max, Molly and Peter looked at Snowy. He *was* dirtier than he was before. Added to the mud on his fur were grass, flowers and tomatoes. Instead of just being brown, he was brown, green, yellow and red.

"You could change his name to Rainbow," suggested Molly.

"What?" said Old Mr Everett.

"He wouldn't get in the bath," explained Max.

"Of course he wouldn't," said Old Mr Everett. "He's a dog. They don't like baths. But you said you'd washed your dog Spotty lots of times so I thought you'd know what to do."

"It was harder than we thought," said Max.

"Spotty's a different kind of dog,"

explained Molly patiently.

"It doesn't matter what breed they are," said Old Mr Everett. "You bath them all the same."

"Not Spotty," said Molly.

"What do you mean, not Spotty? How do you bath him, then?"

"We don't exactly bath him," said Molly. "We put him in the washing machine."

"Washing machine!" Old Mr Everett was outraged. "Put a dog in a... I shall call the RSPCA—"

"He's a cuddly toy," explained Max quickly.

"A cuddly *dog*," corrected Molly, "so it still counts."

"A cuddly dog," repeated Old Mr Everett weakly.

Max realised that Old Mr Everett was not taking the news well. "The bite of an **adder** is very rarely fatal," he said comfortingly.

Old Mr Everett's mouth opened and closed but no words came out.

Molly gently eased the bike out of his hands. "Thanks for mending the **puncture**," she said. "We'll be off now."

SPRAINED AND STRAINED

Max and Molly walked quickly back towards home with Peter squelching behind them.

"Achoo!" sneezed Peter forlornly.

They turned into Laburnum Avenue. They did not notice Peter's mum getting out of the car. She stooped for a few moments to take a peek at her new perm in the side mirror. Then she straightened up. And caught sight of Max and Molly. With Peter.

"What do you think you're doing, Peter?" she shouted across the road. "I've told you not to play with those two!"

"We weren't playing," protested Max. "We were doing some VERY IMPORTANT SCIENTIFIC DISCOVERING. I bet you wouldn't have said Einstein was playing when he discovered relativity."

"Relativity?" repeated Peter's mum. Max nodded. "Before Einstein," he informed her, "nobody knew who their family were."

Peter's mum was briefly taken aback by this news. Molly took the opportunity to push home the point.

"So you see," she stressed, "we weren't playing at all."

But Peter's mum was no longer taken aback. She had noticed the state of her son and she was now advancing towards him. Angrily.

"Peter! You're soaking wet and filthy!" she cried. "And those are *new shorts*. Get inside and up to the bathroom this instant!"

Peter's mum rushed across the garden
to grab Peter. She was so enraged that
she took a shortcut through her best
flowerbed.

Aaarrgghh!

"Your mum's just found our **hole**," said Max, as the three of them watched her fall face-first into a patch of daffodils.

"My ankle!" yelped Peter's mum, struggling to her feet. Some yellow petals had settled into her new perm. "I think it's broken!"

"If you can stand on it, it's probably only sprained," said Max helpfully.

"I'll give you *sprained*," said Peter's mum, limping menacingly towards them.

Max could see that she was not in the best of tempers. "The yellow-bellied sea snake is very aggressive and its venom is highly toxic," he told her.

The information did not have
the soothing effect Max had expected.
If anything, Peter's mum looked **even
more angry.**

"We know you don't like us playing
with Peter, so we'll go home now,"
said Molly, adopting an injured tone.
"Goodbye, Peter."

"Achoo!" said Peter.

TYRED AND EMOTIONAL

Max and Molly arrived back home
to find their dad on the driveway,
looking puzzled.

"Where have you been?" he said.
"And where... Oh, there it is." He'd
spotted Mum's bike which he'd been

looking for. "I still can't find that **puncture repair kit** anywhere."

"You don't need to," said Max.

"We've mended the tyre," said Molly.

"How?"

"With a little help from some very kind people," explained Molly. "And SCIENCE."

"Well," said Dad, with a proud smile. "You really are geniuses. I'm very pleased with you."

"We thought you would be," said Molly.

"So now we can go on our

family bike ride!"

said Max.

"Of course!" said Dad. "I'll just get Mum."

Two minutes later Mum appeared, reluctantly putting on a cycle helmet.

"That chocolate bar will taste better when you get back," Dad told her.

"It was tasting fine before you took it away," said Mum.

And so all four Peskers got on their bicycles and set off at last on a

family bike ride!

As they were leaving Laburnum Avenue, Max and Molly glanced quickly behind them. Coming from different directions, but all heading towards their house, were Mrs Meadows carrying a garden gnome, Derek carrying a spare tyre, Old Mr Everett with Snowy the multicoloured dog, and Peter's mum, limping heavily.

"Let's make it a really long ride, Dad," said Max.

"A really, **really** long ride," said Molly.

The end

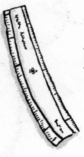

How to Discover Gravity

(WITH A VERY IMPORTANT PARACHUTE EXPERIMENT!)

You will need:

- String
- A small plastic man or a small stuffed toy (like Spotty the dog!)
- Scissors (Careful! No running!)
- A ruler
- An old hanky or a large square piece of plastic cut from a plastic bag

Before you start, tell an adult what you're planning to do. Make sure they're awake first. If they're not, prod them.

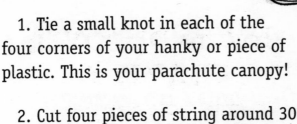

1. Tie a small knot in each of the four corners of your hanky or piece of plastic. This is your parachute canopy!

2. Cut four pieces of string around 30 centimetres long and tie one piece to each corner of your parachute canopy.

3. Tie the four ends of your string in a knot at the bottom and tie the plastic man or stuffed toy at the centre knot with more string.

4. Hold the parachute above your head and drop it. Discover **gravity** at work as it floats gently to the ground! If it doesn't float to the ground you may be on the moon where there isn't any **gravity**. You will need a spaceship.

How to Discover Gravy

(WITH A VERY IMPORTANT RECIPE FOR SAUSAGES AND MASH!)

For 4 people you will need:
- 8 sausages or vegetarian sausages
- 8 potatoes, peeled and cut into chunks
- 1 knob of butter and 1 dash of milk
- 1 jar caramelised onions
- 300ml beef or vegetable stock

Before you start, ask an adult to help you. They will be grumpy otherwise! And nobody likes a grumpy adult.

1. Boil the potatoes in a pan until cooked through. Drain and mash them with the butter and milk until creamy, then set aside to keep warm.

2. Meanwhile, cook the sausages, following the instructions on the packet.

3. For the **gravy**, put the onions and stock into a pan and bring to a simmer.

4. To serve, put a big blob of mash in the middle of each plate and stick two sausages into it. Pour over your delicious **gravy** and eat!

HANNAH SHAW is precisely five foot five inches tall and was born some time in the 1980s. She is the brilliant author and illustrator of a number of picture books, as well an illustrator for young fiction. When she isn't drawing, writing or eating (far too many) chocolate biscuits, Hannah enjoys dog agility, dancing and making robot costumes.

DOMINIC BARKER is not sure how tall he is any more as his doctor tells him

he is shrinking. He has a recurring nightmare in which he is attacked by extremely agile dogs dressed as robots doing the conga. They hit him with chocolate biscuits. Dominic has a good idea who to blame for this...